# Never Bite When a Growl Will Do

Photographs by Michael Nastasi

CHRONICLE BOOKS
SAN FRANCISCO

Library of Congress Cataloging-in-Publication Data:
Nastasi, Michael.
Never bite when a growl will do / photographs
by Michael Nastasi.
p. cm.
ISBN 978-0-8118-4981-4
1. Dogs—Pictorial works. 2. Conduct of life—Quotations, maxims, etc. I. Title.
SF430.N37 2006
636.7'0022'2—dc22
2005012097

Manufactured in Hong Kong.

Designed by Introduction Design
Typeset in Avenir and Caecilia

Photographer's Acknowledgments

Many thanks to my wife, Sue, for her help, support, and love; my mother, for never denying me the three essentials: dogs, art, and love; the fabulous dogs that have shared the daily lives of my wife and me—Mika, Rugby, Minnie, Ellie, Billie, and Dewey; those who encouraged my dog photography, including Joan Young, M. Bari Khan, and Jesper Haynes; Oakley and Aner for patience beyond the call of duty; the great staff at Chronicle Books, including Brooke Johnson; and all the wonderful and inspirational dogs of Central Park—past, present, and future.

10 9 8 7 6 5 4 3 2

Chronicle Books LLC
680 Second Street
San Francisco, California 94107
www.chroniclebooks.com

To err is human,

**to forgive canine.**

Be a **good sport.**

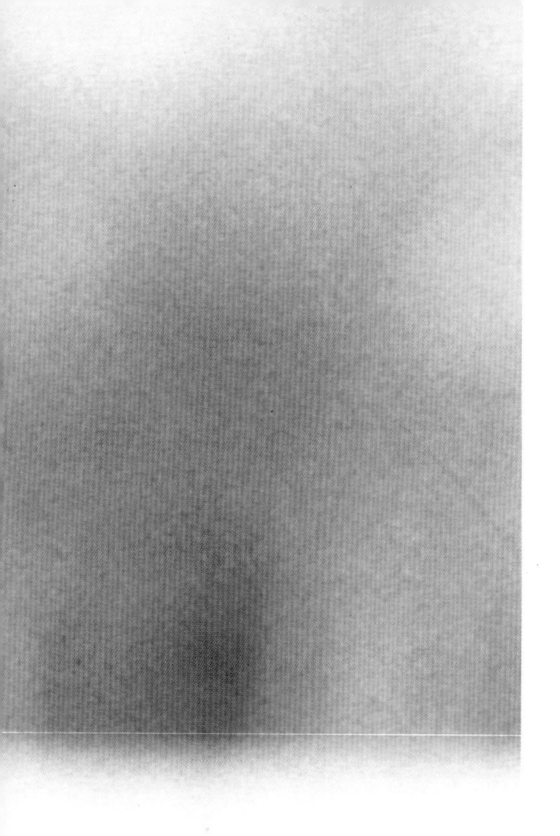

**Persevere** in the face of difficulty.

Always give your friends

**a shoulder to lean on.**

When in doubt,

**sleep on it.**

Life is a game of **give and take.**

It’s okay to be sad sometimes.

Share and share alike.

Let your **feelings show.**

If what you want lies buried, **dig deeper.**

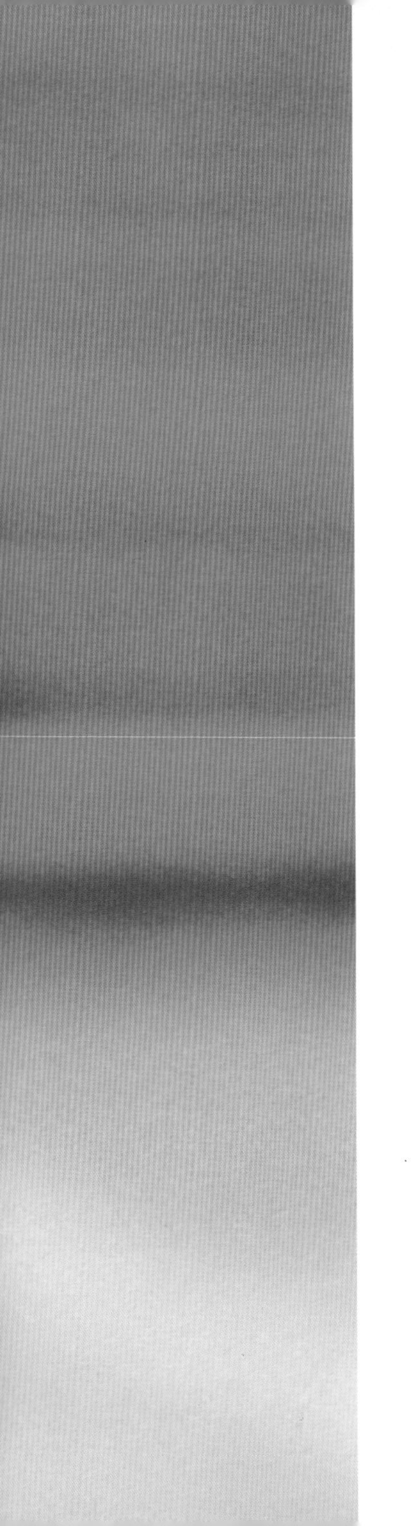

Don't let **anyone** stare you down.

**Lend an ear**

to a friend in need.

Keep your eye **on the ball.**

Be yourself.

When it's in your best interest, **practice obedience.**

**Keep learning** new tricks.

Every day is a good day to

**treat yourself.**

Always stand up

**for your friends.**

Question authority.

Exude confidence.

If you bite off more than you can chew,

**keep chewing.**

Patience is usually rewarded.

Stand your ground.

Romp daily.

Take time to **dream.**

Keep your eyes on the sun—

**you won't see the shadows.**

Laugh.

Bark softly and

**carry a big stick.**

Strive to be **beautiful inside.**

Never underestimate the power of

**looking cute.**

Take on

**new challenges.**

Start every day

**with a song.**

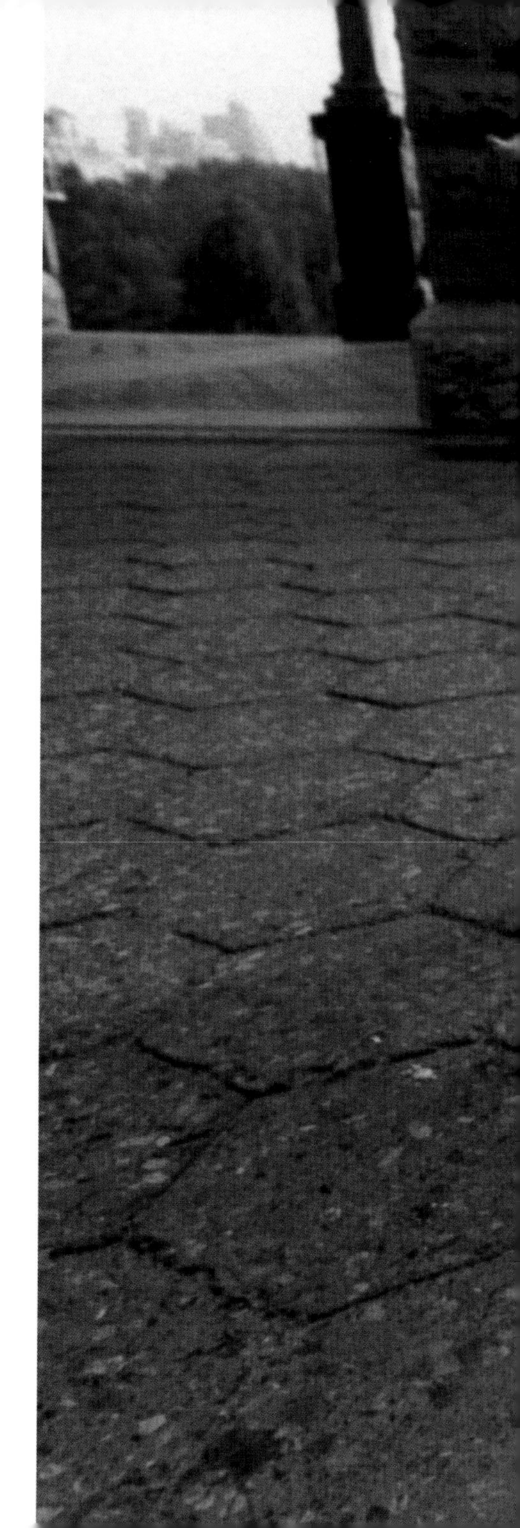

Practice **mindfulness.**

Remember that a bark

**can be bigger than a bite.**

Don't be afraid to **make new friends.**

**Rise**

to every

occasion.

Pick your battles.

Try to

**catch every ball**

thrown your way.

If you've got something to say . . .

## speak up!

Perfect a

firm handshake.

Know thyself.

Let it **all hang out.**

**Take time** to sniff every blade of grass.

Keep a **low profile.**

Never bite
when a growl will do.

And remember—

it's a dog's life.

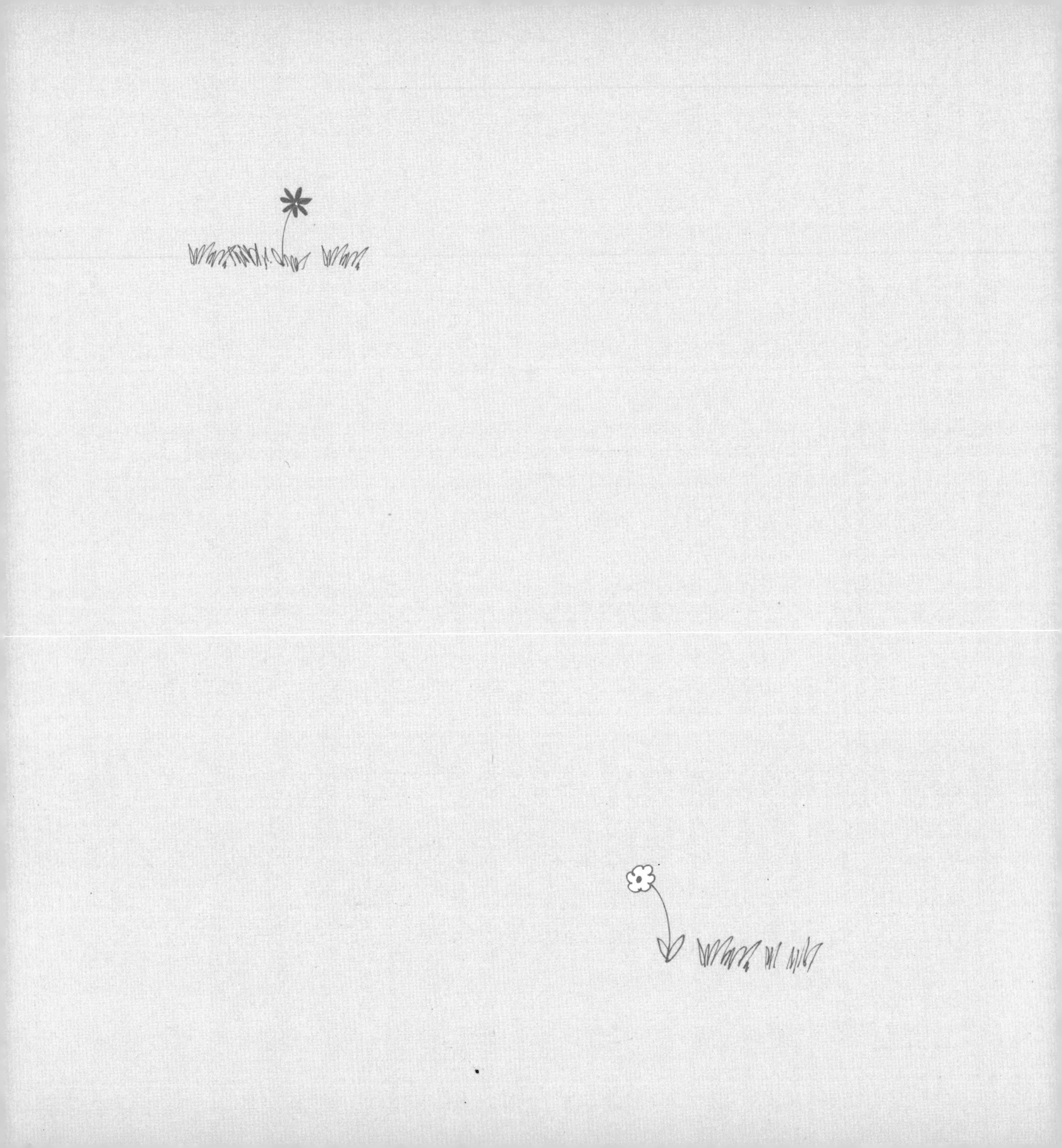